FUZZY-WUZZY WOMBAT
and other rhymes

Natasha Bita

illustrated by Kim Neale

koala
BOOKS

koalabooks.com.au

Sweet giddy sugar glider
Soars between the trees.
Floats above the flowers
With the butterflies and bees!

Whoooop-peeee!

Jumpy joey kangaroo
Cuddles close to mummy,
Happy playing peek-a-boo
And hiding in her tummy!

Boing! Boing! Boing!

Splashy little platypus
Playing hide-and-seek!
Frightening the funny fish
Swimming in the creek.

Peek-a-booooo!

Lizard lazes in the sun,
Then flees in fright —
How fast he runs!
Frilly fellow's very shy.
Never waits to say, 'Bye-bye!'

Eeeeeeeek!

Magpie swoops to guard her nest.
It's there she hides her treasure chest!
Shimmer, glimmer,
Gold and glitter.
Twinkly toys to make her twitter!

Tweet! Tweet! Tweet!

Dilly-dally dingo
Chases pretty butterflies.
Fluffy little puppy
Likes to run and exercise!

Huff-huff-huff-huff!

Lorikeet's a cheeky clown
Who squawks and tweets —
Bobs upside-down.
Such pretty feathers:
Red
Green
Blue
Yellow.
What a noisy little fellow!

Screech!

Fuzzy-wuzzy wombat
Snoozing in the sun,
Wiggling his whiskers
And wobbling his tum!

Zzz

ZZZZZZZZ!

Hungry baby fruit bat
Fills a grumbly tummy,
Gobbling grapes and growing fat.
Fresh figs are really yummy!

Yum -yum -yum!

Emu tries so hard to fly,
Waves her wings
And hops up high,
Flips and flaps...
Oh me! Oh my!
This bird's too big to
reach the sky!

Flip-flap-flip-flap!

Bathtime at the billabong
For smiley crocodile.
Splish-splosh-splashing all day long
And singing all the while!

La-laa-laaa-laaaa!

Kookaburra laughs with glee,
Hoots and chuckles in his tree,
Giggling gladly at a joke.
What a cheerful little bloke!

Ha-ha-
ha-ha-heeee!

Echidna giggles,
Squirms and wriggles.
Her coat of prickles
Really tickles!

Pretty possum plays all night,
Swinging in the treetops,
Singing in the bright moonlight
And dancing on the rooftops!

Cha-cha-cha!

Cuddly koala
Cosy as can be,
Munching yummy gum leaves
And snuggling in a tree!

Shhhhhhhh!!

For Darcy, Lara, Leo & Matteo

Koala Books
www.koalabooks.com.au
First published in Australia in 2007
by Koala Books 4 Merchant Street,
Mascot, Australia, 2020
Reprinted in 2009 and 2012

National Library of Australia CiP data:
Bita, Natasha.
Fuzzy Wuzzy Wombat
and other rhymes.
For children.
ISBN 9780 86461 7156
1. Rhymes - Juvenile fiction.
I. - Neale, Kim. II. Title.
A823.3

Produced by Phoenix Offset. Printed in China.
10 9 8 7 6 5 4 3
14 13 12 11